Octavio and the Hungry Snake

Written by Robert A. Middleton
Illustrations by Rhys Sampson

Dedicated to my two special princesses, Eden and Emma, who love their Daddy's stories.
–R. M.

The pictures of this book are dedicated to my Lollipop Guild.
–R. S.

ISBN 978-1-61225-207-0

Published by Mirror Publishing
Milwaukee, WI 53214

Printed in the USA.

3 1466 01249 9337

There once was a little gray mouse who made his home near the bottom of a great tree. Above his door was a sign that read Octavio's Casa.

Octavio was not like other mice. He knew how to do something that no other mouse in the world could do—he knew how to read! No one really knows how Octavio learned to read, but if you were to ask him, he would tell you that it took lots and lots of practice.

The truth is, Octavio loved to read. In fact, he loved reading books even more than he loved cheese, and that is a lot! Octavio's favorite thing to do—especially on rainy days—was to sit in his most comfortable chair and have some cheese and crackers while reading his favorite books about great adventures. He also read other kinds of books, like the one he had just finished reading called *How to Trick Dangerous Creatures*. This book taught Octavio how to get safely away from creatures that like to eat mice!

"Caramba!" Octavio said, "I am glad I can read, because now I know!"

Yes, there was no doubt about it. Octavio loved to read.

One day, when the warm sun's rays shone through the many leaves of the trees and put small specks of light on the ground, Octavio decided to go on an adventure. So he packed some cheese and crackers into his backpack, closed and locked his door, and set off through the forest.

Octavio walked and walked and walked and only stopped every now and then to have a snack. At last, he came to an area of the forest that he had never seen before.

In the bushes just in front of him he saw two eyes moving closer and closer toward him. When the eyes got close enough, Octavio could see that they belonged to a very large snake! His whiskers stiffened. The fur on the back of his neck stood straight up. His heart jumped. His tail twitched and then stopped. He was as quiet as any mouse ever was!

He stayed perfectly still.

"Caramba! Serpiente grande!" Octavio thought.

The snake hissed and slithered around Octavio in a big circle. Its eyes stared. Its tongue flicked in and out of its mouth, tasting the air. Octavio remembered that snakes do those kinds of things when they are searching for food. It's true. The snake was very hungry. It stopped hissing and slithering and said in a very ssssnaky voice, "You are tressssspassssing in my foressssst!"

"I—I'm sorry amigo," said Octavio's shaky voice, for he knew that snakes could be very dangerous, especially when they were near mice. He wanted to be as polite as possible.

"You didn't know thissss issss my foresssst?" the snake said in a frightening voice.

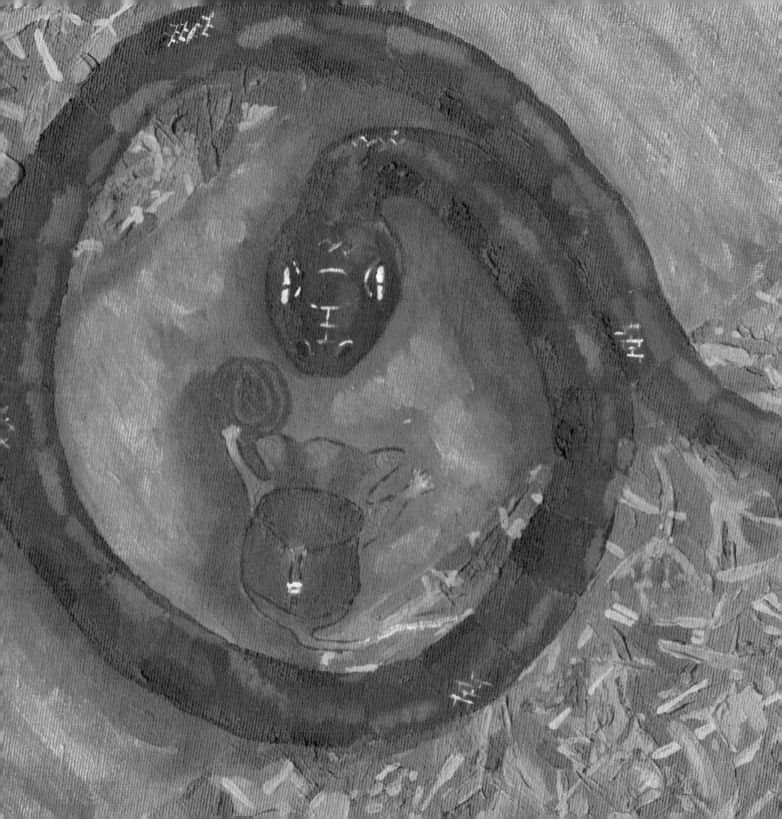

"Why…uh…yes, I do know that this is your forest, amigo. That is why I am trying to be ever so quiet. I would not want to disturb you as I pass by," said Octavio, who was quickly trying to think of a way out of his dangerous situation.

The snake then said, "I have never eaten a gray mouse before. I am curioussss…are you nicccce and juiccccy like the white and brown onessss? You know, I have not eaten for two whole weekssss! I am very hungry, so I think I will have you for my dinner right now!"

As the snake said this, he moved in close to Octavio. Octavio's mind was racing and oh, he was so scared! Then the snake came even closer and opened his mouth, ready to take a bite! Octavio looked at the hungry snake and had an idea. He quickly opened his backpack and took out a bit of cheese and bravely held it in front of him so the snake could see it. The snake stopped and said, "What are you doing?"

"Oh…I was just thinking," said Octavio, "that you are an awfully large snake and I am such a very small mouse. I would not make a good meal for you."

"But I don't like cheesssse," said the snake, "and I would rather jusssst eat you up and be done with it!"

"Wouldn't you rather eat a hundred mice?" Octavio asked, for he remembered reading in his book that snakes are greedy and always try to eat more than they should.

"Yessss, that would be a treat," said the snake, "but you are the only mousssse I ssssee, and ssssinccccce I do not like cheesssse, I believe that I will eat you now!"

Octavio, with his brain still quickly thinking, said, "you don't understand, amigo. This is not just cheese—It's magic cheese!"

"What do you mean, mousssse?" asked the snake.

"This really is magic cheese!" Octavio said. "Did you know that if you plant it in the ground, it will grow into a huge cheese tree in just a few minutes?"

"Why, you don't ssssay!" the snake said.

Now, the snake knew many things about mice. The one thing he knew above all was that mice loved cheese. If he were to plant it as Octavio said, he was sure that when the cheese tree would grow and bloom, it would get hundreds and hundreds of mice to come from all around and he could quickly eat them up!

"Give me that!" said the greedy snake, as he took a bit of cheese from Octavio. "I musssst plant thissss right away!"

The snake slithered off through the forest and Octavio—that clever little mouse—ran as fast as his little mouse feet could carry him!

"Andale! Andale!" said Octavio. He ran and ran and ran through the forest, without stopping, all the way to his casa! He quickly unlocked his door, jumped inside, and shut the door behind him. He was safe at last!

Later that night, it began to rain. Octavio sat in his favorite chair, eating his favorite snack on his favorite kind of night. As he ate his cheese and crackers, Octavio thought about how wonderful it is that we can all learn so many things! We can learn how to tie our shoes, how to be polite and use our manners, and how to play music and dance. He thought about how important it is to learn to read and remember the things we have read.

"What fantastic things our brains are," Octavio said to himself. "We can learn so many wonderful things."

How marvelous it is that we can be very scared, but still have enough courage to do brave things if we put our minds to it. We can even trick a hungry snake once in a while!

THE END

CPSIA information can be obtained
at www.ICGtesting.com
Printed in the USA
BVIC011810160613
323389BV00001B

JUL - 2014

9 781612 252070